Cover illustrated by Marina Fedotova

Phoenix International Publications, Inc.
8501 West Higgins Road, Suite 300, Chicago, Illinois 60631
Lower Ground Floor, 59 Gloucester Place, London W1U 8JJ

www.pikidsmedia.com

8 7 6 5 4 3 2 1

Manufactured in China.

ISBN: 978-1-4508-5854-0

my **LittLe** TReaSuRY

Fairy Tales

pi kids® phoenix international publications, inc.

Contents

Cinderella

Illustrated by Yoshiko Jaeggi
Adapted from the European fairy tale

Many years ago, there lived a beautiful girl who was unlucky enough to have a very mean stepmother. Not only was the stepmother mean, but she also had two daughters who were even meaner than she.

As a result, the poor girl was forced to do all the worst chores in the house. She cooked, cleaned, mended, and even split firewood.

But her least favorite chore was cleaning the ash and cinder out of the fireplace. Although her stepmother wouldn't let her wear nice clothes, the rags she did wear got filthy when she cleaned the fireplace.

"Look at you, all covered in cinders," teased her stepsisters. "Ha! Ha! Look at dirty little Cinderella!"

And so it went; poor Cinderella would spend her days cooking and cleaning and her nights tending to her sisters' hair, dresses, and shoes.

One day a messenger arrived with a very important delivery. It was an invitation to the prince's royal ball.

"Oooh!" squealed one of the mean stepsisters. "I hope the handsome prince asks me to dance with him!"

"He will surely ask me," said the other stepsister. "I am the most beautiful young lady in all the kingdom!"

"I know the prince will be enchanted by both of you," declared their mother. "You are both lucky to be blessed with my good looks — unlike our little Cinderella."

The three women turned to look at poor Cinderella, teasing her for being dirty.

When the night of the ball arrived, the stepsisters squeezed into their gowns, forcing Cinderella to help them. All the while, they scolded her and taunted her because she would not be going to the ball.

"Ouch! You are pulling my hair!" yelled one stepsister.

"While we are dancing with the prince, Cinderella will still be here tidying the house," laughed the other.

Cinderella watched sadly as they left for the ball. When she was alone, Cinderella sat down in the garden and sobbed.

"If only I could go and dance at the ball!" she cried.

The very next instant a flash lit up the garden. From out of nowhere there appeared a winged woman dressed in a flowing gown.

"Who are you?" asked Cinderella with apprehension.

"I am your fairy godmother," the woman answered. "I am here to help you. I have come to bring you the good fortune you deserve. Tonight is the night of the royal ball, is it not? Would you like to go?"

"Oh, goodness! Yes!" said Cinderella.

"Well, then," the fairy godmother said, "let's get you presentable, shall we?"

With a wave of her wand, the fairy showered the garden with sparks. When Cinderella opened her eyes, she was amazed by what she saw.

"Why, my rags have turned into a beautiful gown!" said Cinderella. "And the pumpkin and mice have become a coach and a team of fine horses!"

"You must hurry," said the fairy godmother. "The magic won't last. My spell will be broken at the exact moment that the clock strikes midnight!"

And with that, the stunning Cinderella was whisked away to the ball.

"Who is that girl?" asked one of the guests as Cinderella entered the ball. "She must be royalty."

The prince spotted Cinderella and immediately asked her to dance. She blushed slightly, but offered her hand.

"Who does that girl think she is?" cried
the two stepsisters, not knowing the stranger
was really Cinderella.

As the night wore on, the prince
danced only with Cinderella.

"This night has been one of
the most wonderful of my life,"
Cinderella told him. She could tell
they were falling in love.

"Who are you?" he asked.
Before Cinderella could
reply, the clock began to strike
twelve. It was midnight! She
had forgotten all about her
fairy godmother's warning!

"I must get home," she thought. "I cannot let the prince see me in my rags."

And so she turned and ran away.

"Come back!" cried the startled prince. "You did not even tell me your name!"

But Cinderella did not hear him, for she was already out of the palace doors. In her hurry, she lost one of the beautiful glass slippers her fairy godmother had given her.

The prince rushed after the girl, but to no avail. However, he did find the single glass slipper that she had left behind. As he bent to pick it up, a single tear slid down his cheek.

The next day, Cinderella was again in her rags, cleaning her stepmother's house. As she scrubbed, she heard her stepsisters talking excitedly. "The prince is searching the entire kingdom for the girl he loves," said one.

"He has her glass slipper with him. Whomever it fits, he will marry," said the other stepsister.

When the prince arrived at their house, Cinderella watched, hidden in a corner, as her stepsisters tried on the slipper. But their feet were far too big for the delicate shoe.

The prince was standing to leave when he spotted Cinderella. "Won't you try on the slipper?" asked the prince.

"Dirty Cinderella?" laughed the wicked stepmother. "She is not the girl you love!"

But the prince insisted. Sure enough, Cinderella's foot fit perfectly inside the glass slipper. He looked past the ash-stained face and into Cinderella's eyes — it was her, all right. The prince had found his love at last!

The couple rushed off to be married at once. They lived happily ever after.

Rapunzel

Illustrated by Kathi Ember
Adapted from the Grimm Brothers' fairy tale

 here once lived a young couple that was expecting their first child. One evening, the wife had a craving for the delicious rapunzel lettuce that grew in the garden of their neighbor. As it happened, their neighbor was a bitter and evil old witch.

But the young husband didn't want to let down his lovely wife, so he ran outside and jumped into the garden.

Just as he knelt to pick a head of lettuce, the witch appeared.

"How dare you enter my garden!" screeched the witch. "And how dare you attempt to steal my lettuce!"

"I meant no harm," said the man. "I merely wanted to treat my wife to a delicious evening supper. Please don't hurt me; I'm to be a father soon!"

"Go home," said the witch. "Take all that you want from my garden. But when your child comes, I shall take her for my own!"

The scared man climbed back over the garden wall and hurried home, his pockets full of rapunzel lettuce. When he got there, he did not tell his wife what had happened.

A short time later, a baby girl was born. The woman named her child Rapunzel, after her favorite food. Later that day, there was a knock on the door. It was the witch!

When the husband explained what had happened, the young couple realized that there was nothing they could do. The witch took the baby and left.

To prevent the girl's parents from finding her, the witch locked Rapunzel away in a tall tower. Though they searched near and far, Rapunzel's parents were never able to find their little girl.

Many years passed, and Rapunzel grew into a beautiful young woman. During her time in the tower, Rapunzel had never been allowed to cut her hair, so it had grown long.

The window to Rapunzel's room
was very high, so to reach it, the witch
would yell, "Rapunzel! Rapunzel!
Throw down your golden hair!"

Rapunzel would obey, and the
witch would scurry up the two
golden braids.

One day, a handsome prince
passing through town heard
a girl's voice singing a lovely
song. He was following
the sound of the glorious
voice when suddenly he
heard a scratchy voice
begin to croak.

22

"Rapunzel! Rapunzel!" growled the voice. "Throw down your golden hair!"

Through his spyglass, the prince saw a beautiful girl with long golden hair. She was perched in a tower window. He spotted an ugly old witch climbing up her golden braids.

The handsome prince waited until the old witch left the tower. Enchanted by the beautiful girl, the prince crept up to the tower and called, "Rapunzel! Rapunzel! Throw down your golden hair!"

As he expected, two golden braids of hair fell from the window. Taking hold of them, the prince climbed up the tower wall, where he reached the girl.

"I am Rapunzel," she began to explain as the prince climbed through the window. "An old witch took me from my parents when I was but a baby. I have lived locked in this tower ever since."

"You shall not have to endure another day here," said the prince.

He climbed down the tower wall to the ground below. There he stood while Rapunzel leaped from the window into his arms.

Then the two of them quickly hid behind a shrub just as the bitter and evil old witch arrived.

"Rapunzel! Rapunzel! Throw down your golden hair!" said the witch.

When the braids never fell, the witch realized that Rapunzel had escaped. The witch was beyond furious and stormed off into the forest, defeated.

Once they were certain they were safe from the witch, the prince helped Rapunzel onto his horse, and away they rode.

After riding for some time, the prince and Rapunzel finally arrived at the home of her parents. It had been many years since the witch had stolen their child, but the poor couple had never forgotten their daughter.

Rapunzel's heart swelled with love the moment she laid eyes on her parents' careworn faces.

"I am your daughter, Rapunzel," said the girl. "This brave prince was able to rescue me from the old witch who took me from you all those years ago. He would like for us to come live in his castle."

And that is exactly what they did! Lovely Rapunzel and the prince were wed, and everyone lived happily ever after.

Little Red Riding Hood

Illustrated by Thea Kliros
Adapted from the European fairy tale

 In a small town next to a large forest, there lived a little girl. She was called Little Red Riding Hood because of the cape her grandmother had made for her.

One day Red Riding Hood's mother said, "Grandmother is sick. Take her this basket of fresh goodies. Just be sure that you stay on the path."

Little Red Riding Hood soon forgot her mother's warning. She wandered off the path and immediately met a wolf.

"Where are you going, little girl?" asked the wolf. "What do you have in that basket?"

"I am going to visit my grandmother, who lives in the house with the red door," answered the girl. "She is sick, and I am taking her a basket of treats."

"Tell me, do you have any fresh strawberries in your basket?" asked the wolf.

"No," admitted Red Riding Hood. "But my grandmother loves strawberries. I will run and pick some right now."

"You can leave your basket with me," suggested the hungry wolf. "I'd be happy to watch it for you while you are gone."

"No, thank you," said Red Riding Hood. "I'll need it so I can carry the strawberries."

The wolf watched Little Red Riding Hood hurry away. While Red Riding Hood was off collecting berries, the wolf came up with a plan and quickly scurried about the forest.

"I see that you do not have flowers for your grandmother," the wolf said when Red Riding Hood returned. "I have just picked this bouquet for my own grandmother. I suggest you pick one, too."

Little Red Riding Hood thought that was a good idea. But as she began her search for flowers, she was too distracted to notice the wolf run off in the direction of Grandmother's little house.

Little Red Riding
Hood gathered her bouquet of
flowers and skipped off to deliver her
gifts. At the same time, the wolf sneaked
into Grandmother's house. He frightened
her so greatly that she ran right out the
front door!

Then the wolf dressed in one of
Grandmother's nightgowns. He put
on a sleeping bonnet and slipped into
Grandmother's comfortable bed to wait for
Little Red Riding Hood.

The wolf did not have to wait long. In a
moment he heard the front door open.

"Hello, Grandmother," called Little Red
Riding Hood. "I brought you a basket of
goodies from Mother and me."

"Thank you, my dear," said the wolf with
a disguised voice. "That is most kind. I am
feeling better now. Your basket of goodies
certainly smells delicious. Please, come closer,
and give me some news from the village."

Little Red Riding Hood stepped closer to
the bed. But something seemed different. Her
grandmother looked very strange!
The girl was surprised to see that
her grandmother's eyes
looked much larger
than she remembered.

"Why, Grandmother," said Little Red
Riding Hood, "what big eyes you have!"

The wolf blinked, trying to hide them
from her. "All the better to see you with,
my dear," he said.

As the wolf shifted in the bed to hide his
eyes, the bonnet slipped from his head.

"Why, Grandmother," said Little Red
Riding Hood, "what big ears you have!"

"All the better to hear you with, my dear," said the wolf as he fixed the bonnet, letting the covers slip from his face.

"Why, Grandmother," said Little Red Riding Hood, "what big *teeth* you have!"

"All the better to EAT you with!" cried the wolf.

With that, Little Red Riding Hood let out a scream and ran from the room. The wolf gave chase with hunger in his eyes.

"Stop!" cried a loud voice.

Little Red Riding Hood looked up to see a woodcutter holding his ax in the air. He reached for the wolf and grabbed him by the tail. Then the woodcutter carried the wolf into the forest.

Grandmother came running up to Little

Red Riding Hood. She had been hiding in the garden shed.

"Grandmother! I am so glad you are safe!" cried Little Red Riding Hood. "I was worried that the wolf had eaten you."

Grandmother gave Little Red Riding Hood a great big hug as the woodcutter came out of the woods.

"I do not think that wolf will trouble you again," he said, adjusting his cap.

"Thank you," said Grandmother. "Won't you please join us for a snack?"

The woodcutter, Little Red Riding Hood, and Grandmother sat and enjoyed the basket of delicious goodies.

Now when Red Riding Hood visits her grandmother, she is careful to stay on the path.

Jack and the Beanstalk

Illustrated by Sue Williams
Adapted from the English fairy tale

There was once a poor widow who lived with her son, Jack. They made a meager living selling milk. That is, until their cow went dry. Jack's mother asked him to take the cow and sell her for a good price.

On his way to market, Jack met a man who asked him where he was taking the cow.

"I am going to sell her," he said.

"You look like a sharp young man," said the stranger. "I will give you these four magic beans for your cow."

"Magic beans?" Jack was delighted with the offer. He swiftly made the trade and hurried home.

"Look what I got in exchange for the cow!" he said eagerly.

"You foolish boy!" cried Jack's mother, tossing the beans out the window. "Now we must go to bed hungry."

When Jack
awoke the next
morning, he noticed an
odd shadow on his window.
He ran outside to find that a
huge beanstalk had sprung up
during the night! It was so tall
that the top disappeared
into the clouds.

Jack was a very
curious boy, and
decided to climb
the beanstalk. He
climbed up it to
the very top.

Jack could not believe his eyes! In front of him stood an enormous, magnificent castle.

Since his arms and legs felt so tired and sore, Jack knew that the long climb up the beanstalk had not been a dream. He rubbed his eyes to make sure he was not seeing things, but the castle still stood before him.

Curious as ever, Jack decided to walk to the castle. As he strolled, he met a beautiful fairy who told Jack the tale of the giant who lived there and how greedy he was. She also told him how, long ago, the terrible giant had stolen all of Jack's father's gold.

The fairy told Jack that the gold was his birthright and he should take it back.

Jack reached the steps of the castle and made his way to the kitchen, where he saw the giant asleep at a table. The giant had been counting gold coins when he nodded off.

Jack climbed onto the table and grabbed a bag of gold. But as he climbed down, the giant awoke.

The giant sniffed the air
and roared, "Fee-fi-fo-fum!
I smell the blood of an Englishman!"
Frightened, Jack gripped the bag
tightly and raced out of the castle as fast
as his little feet would carry him.

The giant gave chase, but Jack was
fast. He lost the giant just as he
threw the bag down to his
mother's garden. Jack's
mother was overcome
with joy. She knew that
she and Jack would
never go hungry
ever again!

Wanting to take back all
that the giant had stolen from
his family, Jack climbed the
beanstalk once again. This
time, he ran into the giant's
wife. She was wary of helping
Jack, but the little boy was so
polite she could not resist.

Jack hid in the oven
when the giant came
looking for his supper.
"Fee-fi-fo-fum, I
smell the blood of
an Englishman!"
roared the giant.

"Don't be silly, love," said the giant's wife. "It is only your supper."

The giant ate his meal and then he told his wife to bring him his hen.

Jack peeked out of the oven as he heard the giant shout, "Lay!"

On command, the hen laid a golden egg!

Jack waited patiently until the giant fell asleep, then he leaped from the oven, snatched the hen, and raced out of the castle. He hurried back down the beanstalk to his mother's house to show her what he had gotten this time.

After quite some time had passed, Jack decided to climb the beanstalk once more. Jack sneaked back into the castle, and this time he hid in a large pot.

The giant wandered into the kitchen and was about to peek into Jack's pot when his wife called him to supper, saving Jack again.

After eating, the giant called for his magic harp. The harp began to play the most enchanting music Jack had ever heard.

Before long, the giant was lulled to sleep by the music. When Jack heard the giant begin to snore, he knew it was safe to climb out of the pot. He grabbed the harp and started to run away.

"Master! Master!" cried the harp. The giant awoke with a start. Jack held tightly onto the harp as he ran for his life.

Jack could hear the *thump, thump* of the giant's footsteps behind him. He knew the giant took large steps, so Jack ran faster than he ever had before. Luckily, the giant had just eaten supper and was a bit sluggish.

By now, Jack was an expert at climbing up and down the beanstalk. Even with the harp, he slid skillfully around stems and leaves. As Jack climbed down, he called to his mother.

"Mother! Hurry! Bring me the ax!" he shouted.

When Jack reached the ground, the giant was only halfway down the beanstalk. Jack took the ax and began to hack away, chopping at the beanstalk as fast as he could as the giant got closer.

Finally, Jack swung the ax mightily one last time and cut the beanstalk in two. The beanstalk, and giant, crashed to the ground.

Jack had successfully retrieved all of his father's treasure and saved everyone from the terrible giant in the clouds. Jack's mother was very proud of him. And the two of them, the hen, and the harp lived happily ever after.

Hansel and Gretel

Illustrated by Doug Klauba
Adapted from the Grimm Brothers' fairy tale

 ansel and Gretel lived in a cottage at the edge of the forest. Their father was a simple woodcutter, and although he worked hard, the family was very poor. Many times Hansel and Gretel had nothing but a crust of bread for their supper.

At night, after they were in bed, their parents would speak in worried voices.

Even though
they whispered,
Hansel and Gretel
could hear what
they said.

"I must go
into the forest to find
work," Father sighed. "It will be dangerous,
but it's the only way."

Mother gasped. Father was too old to
work in the forest. The children discussed
this in their room.

"Hansel, we simply can't let Father go,"
whispered Gretel to her brother from her
bed. "What can we do?"

After a moment
of thought, Hansel
said, "I will travel into
the forest instead."

"Then I will come with you," said Gretel.
"You may need my help."

Before daylight, Hansel and Gretel crept
out of their beds and pulled on their clothes.
Hansel collected some bread from the
kitchen and stuffed it into his pockets.

The children walked silently. They
walked all day long until their feet hurt and
their legs felt tired and heavy.

"I did not realize the forest was so big,"
Gretel said.

"Nor did I," said Hansel. "But don't worry. I have made sure we will not get lost. I left a trail of bread crumbs behind us, in case we need to turn back."

"You are very clever, Hansel," Gretel said. "But look!"

Gretel pointed behind them. Hansel saw three blackbirds carefully eating each bread crumb he had dropped. The trail was gone!

Hansel stared where his trail had been. How would they find their way home?

By now the children were very tired, but they continued to walk through the forest. Surely they would come across someplace they could rest, or someone who would offer them something small to eat. They were certainly lost now.

Night fell upon the forest, and strange noises came from behind the trees. Hansel and Gretel sat down near a tree and huddled against the cold. After a short time, they both managed to fall asleep, dreaming of a warm supper.

In the morning they continued to walk. After a while, the children entered a small clearing. They could not believe their eyes.

"Gretel, look!" Hansel shouted. "A cottage!"

"Maybe whoever lives there will have something to eat," said Gretel.

As the children hurried closer, they saw that this was no ordinary cottage. Its walls were made of gingerbread, and its windows of crystal clear sugar.

The children knocked on the door. When it opened, an old woman with a cane came out.

"We have been traveling alone through the forest," Gretel said. "We are very tired and so hungry. May we rest here?"

The old woman invited the children inside. She made them a delicious meal, then gave them soft beds on which to rest.

But in the morning, the old woman grabbed Hansel and locked him in a cage.

"I am a witch," the woman said. "You will be my supper, once you are nice and fat."

For the next few weeks, the witch made sure Hansel had plenty to eat. Each day the witch would stand by Hansel's cage and say, "Stick out your finger so I can see how plump you are!"

But Hansel was a clever boy. He knew that witches are nearly blind, so rather than let the old woman feel his finger, Hansel held out a small, thin chicken bone that Gretel had sneaked to him. The trick worked perfectly!

"Hmmm," the witch would say, feeling the chicken bone. "What a scrawny thing you are! You must eat more!"

One morning, the witch ordered Gretel to fetch some water. "Whether Hansel is fat or lean," she said, "today I will cook and eat him! I have waited too long."

"No!" Gretel shouted.

"You stubborn child, do as I say," the witch demanded impatiently.

The witch nudged Gretel up to the oven. "Check the oven to make sure it is hot."

"No," Gretel said. She knew better than
to trust a witch. "I don't know how to check."

"Then I will do it myself!" said the witch.
Just as she leaned over, Gretel gave her
a push. The witch fell right into the oven.
Gretel slammed the iron door shut and
bolted it so the witch could not get out.

Gretel quickly released Hansel
from his cage. With nothing else
to fear, the children sat down
and enjoyed a feast.

Before they left, the
children gathered
food to eat during
their long journey.

As they wandered
through the house searching for food,
Hansel and Gretel discovered boxes of
pearls and precious stones. They stuffed
their pockets with jewels and filled large
sacks with as much food as they could.

The children set off through the forest.
After days of walking, the children came to
a place in the woods that looked familiar.
Suddenly, they could see their own little
cottage through the trees!

The children began to run.
"Mother, Father! We
are home at last!"
they shouted.

When Mother and Father
heard their calls, they ran to
meet them. They hugged Hansel
and Gretel for a very long time.

"Look what we have brought," said
Hansel. He took the jewels from his pockets
and laid them on the table. "We will never be
hungry again."

"You are very good and brave children,"
said Father. "But you must promise me that
you will never run away again."

"We promise," they said together. And
the family lived happily ever after.

Sleeping Beauty

Illustrated by Holly Jones
Adapted from the European fairy tale

nce upon a time, a beloved queen gave birth to a beautiful daughter. A great festival was planned. Deep in a dark forest of the same kingdom, there lived a wicked witch who led a lonely life. "Bah!" cried the bitter witch. "I'll put a stop to all these cheers!"

With evil in her heart, the witch set out for the castle.

The moment she arrived, the cruel witch cast a terrible spell on the princess.

"On her nineteenth birthday," hissed the witch, "the princess will prick her finger upon a spinning wheel. This will cause her to fall into a deep sleep — forever!"

Exactly nineteen years later, the princess prepared for her birthday party by sewing a dress for herself. True to the witch's word, however, the princess pricked her finger.

The princess instantly
fell into a deep sleep. The
queen was horrified to find
her daughter fast asleep on
the floor of the sewing room.
She knew at once what had
happened. The princess
was brought to her own
room and put to bed.

The
princess
lay in bed
as the queen
set out to find
some help.

It seemed that no one could help the sleeping princess — until one day when a fairy arrived at the castle.

"I have hopeful news about your daughter," the fairy told the queen.

In her travels, the fairy had met a bitter old witch who bragged about her powerful spells. The sneering witch had mentioned the one thing that could break her formidable sleeping spell. The queen listened.

"True love," the fairy told the queen. "If a man of pure heart falls in love with the princess, she will awaken from her sleep."

"What man would fall in love with a sleeping girl?" asked the queen, sighing. "All hope is surely lost."

"To bring you comfort," said the fairy, "I can cast a spell on your kingdom so you may all share in her slumber. When the princess awakens, so too will you."

The queen was silent.

"I agree to this plan,"
she answered, finally. "Now,
kind fairy, cast your spell."

And so she did.

A hundred years passed
as a dense forest grew
around the castle. It was
then that a handsome
prince discovered the
hidden kingdom.
As he entered,
he saw that a
guard was
sound asleep. In
fact, everyone was asleep.

The prince walked through a great hall, finding more sleeping people with every step.

"Wake up!" he cried, but it was no use. Soon, the prince found the princess's room. The prince gazed at her face. She was so peaceful and so lovely. Overcome with emotion, the prince stepped to the girl's bedside, lifted her hand softly, and gently kissed it.

The princess's eyes opened in a flash. She looked at the young man sitting beside her.

"It's you!" she said. "You have come to me at last! I waited for you in my dream. A kind fairy told me you would come!"

At that moment, the queen and her sleeping subjects awoke as well. As they all celebrated, the queen rushed to the princess's room.

"My daughter!" she said, overjoyed. "You have come back to me!"

The queen looked at the prince. He was the man of pure heart whom the fairy had so clearly described.

"Thank you," she said, embracing him. "Thank you! You have saved my daughter and my kingdom!"

As the people throughout the castle woke from their slumber, they rubbed the sleep of a hundred years from their eyes. Word spread quickly that the princess had found her prince.

The queen presented the young prince to her subjects. She beamed with pride.

"This man loves my daughter," said the queen, "and they will be married as soon as possible. Let us not waste another moment!"

In a few short days, the sound of wedding bells rang throughout the kingdom. The princess and her prince were married in the grandest ceremony imaginable. The prince, his heart filled with love, had never been happier. The princess had truly found the man of her dreams, and they lived happily ever after.

The Selfish Giant

Illustrated by David Lupton
Adapted from the fairy tale by Oscar Wilde

nce there was a beautiful garden. It was covered with soft grass, colorful flowers, and peach trees ripe with pink blossoms in spring and plump fruit in fall.

Each day, on their way home from school, groups of children would visit the garden. They would lie in the cool grass and hide among the trees. They would pick flowers for their mothers and eat the sweet peaches for a snack. How happy they were!

What the children didn't know was that the garden actually belonged to a giant! This particular giant had taken a vacation, leaving his garden unattended for seven years.

But then one day, out of the blue, the giant returned to find kids in his garden.

"What are you doing here?" he cried in a gruff voice. "This is my garden. Nobody can play here but me!"

To make his point clear, the giant locked the gate and nailed two sturdy planks of wood across the doorway. Then he hung a sign that said: "KEEP OUT!"

The children watched the giant sadly. Now the children had nowhere to play.

Soon spring turned to summer, and summer became fall. Then fall gave way to winter. When winter said farewell, spring came again. Everywhere the land was filled with birds and blossoms. Everywhere, that is, except the selfish giant's garden.

The birds refused to sing there, since no children would hear their songs. Similarly, the trees refused to blossom. A thick coat of snow remained on the ground.

"I cannot understand why spring is so late in coming," said the giant, as he looked out at his cold, white garden. "I hope it will come soon."

But spring never came, nor summer.

One morning, though, a strange thing happened. The giant was lying in bed when he heard a song that sounded so sweet to his ears that he thought he must be dreaming. But it was really a bluebird singing outside his window. It had been so long since he had heard a bird sing in his garden that it seemed to him the most beautiful music in the world.

The selfish giant sat up and looked out the window. What do you think he saw?

It was a most wonderful sight. The kids had crept into the garden through a hole in the wall. The trees were so happy to have them back again that they had covered themselves with pink and white blossoms.

The giant's heart melted as he looked out. "How selfish I have been!" he cried. "Now I know why spring would not come."

He was very sorry for what he had done.

The giant crept downstairs and slowly opened the door. As he entered the garden, he saw that in one corner it was still winter. A little boy stood beneath a tree, stretching his arms up to reach its high branches. The poor tree was still quite covered with frost, and although it bent its branches as low as it could, the boy was too small to reach them.

The giant smiled at the boy and lifted him gently into the tree. The tree broke into bloom as the boy smiled shyly at the giant.

"Does this mean we may play in your garden?" asked the little boy.

"From now on, this is your garden," answered the giant. "You and your friends may come and play whenever you wish."

Every day, the children returned to play. They brought friends, sisters, and brothers. It truly became a place for all children.

Being selfish had made the giant lonely. But when he learned to share, friends filled his garden, and happiness filled his heart.

To this day, the giant can be seen playing with the children in the enchanted garden. The trees and the birds make it pleasant, but it's the children that make it magical.

Goldilocks and the Three Bears

Illustrated by David Merrell
Adapted from the fairy tale by Robert Southey

 nce upon a time there was a cottage in a forest that belonged to a family of bears: Papa Bear, Mama Bear, and wee Baby Bear.

Each morning the three bears made their beds, tidied their house, and ate their breakfast together at the table.

One particular morning, Mama Bear
made a breakfast of piping-hot porridge.
It was so piping hot, in fact, that the three
bears decided to take a walk while their
breakfast cooled.

Just then, a young girl named
Goldilocks came upon the cottage.

"Mmmm," said the girl, "I believe I
smell fresh porridge! Perhaps I will sneak
into this cottage and have just a bite or two."

Goldilocks sneaked into the empty cottage and took a seat at the kitchen table. She took a bite of Papa Bear's porridge, but it was too hot. She took a bite of Mama Bear's porridge, but it was too cold. Then she took a bite of Baby Bear's porridge, and it was so good she ate it all!

The hearty breakfast left Goldilocks feeling very full. She hoped she might find a comfortable chair in the cottage in which to relax.

Goldilocks sat down on Papa Bear's chair, but it was too hard. Mama Bear's chair was too soft. Then she sat down on Baby Bear's chair, and it was just right — until it broke with a loud *SNAP!*

Needing somewhere new to nap, Goldilocks found the bears' beds. Papa Bear's bed was too firm. Mama Bear's bed was too squishy. But Baby Bear's bed was just right!

It didn't take long for Goldilocks to fall fast asleep. Little did she know, however, that at that exact moment the bear family was finishing their morning walk. Certain that their porridge would be cool enough to eat, Papa Bear, Mama Bear, and Baby Bear sat down at the table for breakfast.

"Hmmm," Papa Bear growled, "it seems that someone has been eating my porridge!"

"Oh, don't be silly," replied Mama Bear. But then she looked down at her own porridge.

"Heavens to Betsy!" muttered Mama Bear. "It seems that someone has been eating my porridge, too!"

It isn't every day that one finds one's breakfast has been eaten by someone else. But this did not matter to Baby Bear, who had become quite hungry from taking such a long morning walk. It was as if he hadn't heard his mother or father complain about their porridge.

"Oh, dear!" Baby Bear cried as he looked at his bowl. "It seems that someone has been eating my porridge — and has eaten it all up!"

Upset that their breakfast had been mysteriously tasted and devoured, the three bears went into their living room.

Papa Bear went to his big, hard wooden chair and sat down, but something wasn't right.

"What?" he roared, jumping up from his seat. "Someone has been sitting in my chair!"

Mama Bear was sure that her husband was just being silly. That is, until she sat down in her own chair.

"Gracious!" she declared. "It seems that someone has been sitting in my chair, too!"

Baby Bear was still forlorn from finding his porridge all eaten up. He was so forlorn, in fact, that he didn't hear his parents' complaints. With a frown and a pout, he flopped onto the spot where his small chair had been.

"Eek!" Baby Bear squealed. "Someone has been sitting in my little chair — and has smashed it all to bits and pieces!"

"Eaten porridge! Broken chairs," said Papa Bear. "What is happening here?"

The three bears decided that a quiet nap would help them all relax.

"Wait," announced Papa Bear. "First Baby Bear's porridge was eaten, then his little chair was broken. Let's all check his little bed before we retire to our own rooms."

The bears entered Baby Bear's bedroom.

"Papa!" cried Baby Bear. "Someone is sleeping in my bed!"

Sure enough, there was a small, blond-haired girl napping in Baby Bear's bed. The bears just stared in shock.

It was at that moment that Goldilocks woke up. When she saw the three large bears looking down at her, she was so frightened that she leaped out of the window!

Goldilocks ran away as fast as she could. She never went back into that part of the forest again. And she never, ever ate another bite of porridge.

Rumpelstiltskin

Illustrated by David Hohn
Adapted from the Grimm Brothers' fairy tale

Once there was a poor miller who had a beautiful daughter. A remarkable turn of events one day allowed the miller to meet the king. The miller used this opportunity to tell the king, who was a bachelor, all about his daughter, Sophia.

In his excitement to convince the king to meet his daughter, the man claimed she could spin ordinary straw into gold!

In truth, Sophia had no idea how to spin straw into gold. But the king asked her to come to the palace. He showed her to a room filled with straw and asked her to spin it all into gold by the next day.

Sophia began to cry.

Then, from out of nowhere, a little man appeared. "Why are you crying?" he asked.

The young woman explained.

"I can spin this straw into gold for you," he said. "But you must give me your necklace in return for my favor."

The miller's daughter agreed, and the tiny man set to work. Soon the young woman fell asleep. When she awoke, the room was full of golden thread. The king was very pleased.

"This is a most remarkable talent you have," he said. "If you can repeat what you have done by tomorrow, I will make you my queen."

Convinced she would be found out this time, Sophia began to cry. Once again, the little man appeared.

"I can help you out once again," he said.

The little man paused before saying, "This time, however, you must give me your firstborn child."

Sophia's heart sank. How could she make such a promise? But in her desperation, she agreed.

The odd little man set to work, and the young woman fell asleep. She awoke to find the straw spun into gold.

When the king arrived he was amazed, and asked her to marry him.

"On one condition," she said. "You must never ask me to spin straw into gold again."

The king agreed, and soon he and Sophia were wed.

Though at first the new queen thought that her husband was a bit greedy, she soon found him to be a sweet and caring man, and a noble king. They grew to love each other very much.

When their first child was born, the queen was so happy that she forgot all about her promise to the little man.

Then he appeared.

"Your Highness," said the little man, "I have come to claim what is mine. Your son belongs to me."

"Surely you will not take my child," said the queen. "I was a fool to make such a promise. Now that I am queen, I can give you anything you desire."

"I can see how much you care for your son," he said. "Therefore, I will give you a chance to keep him. If you can guess my name, I will forgive your promise. You have two days."

With that, he was gone.

Queen Sophia quickly ordered one of her porters to follow him. The porter watched the man as he traveled deep into the forest. He set up camp, built a fire, and danced around it.

Meanwhile, the queen compiled a list. She sent for her royal advisers and asked them for the most unusual names they could find. They scoured the countryside and reported their findings to the queen.

The next day, the queen's porter returned to the castle. He had very little to report. The little man had danced around his fire all night long, but he had not spoken a word.

Suddenly, a voice startled the queen.

"Have you any guesses for me, Your Highness?" asked the little man. He had appeared from out of nowhere.

"Indeed, I do," she said. "Are you called Monty? Mal? Montivecchio? Orton? Opyrus? Orenthal? Or perhaps you are Balthazar? Bitmillymont? Bugleheim?"

The queen read every name from her list.

"All of your guesses are wrong!" said the little man. "You have one more day."

The queen again asked her porter to stay with the little man. The porter followed him to the same spot, deep in the forest. And just as he had the night before, the man began to dance around his fire. This time, however, he sang a little song as he danced.

The queen's heart will surely break,
For tomorrow her child I'll take.
But now we play a guessing game,
And Rumpelstiltskin is my name!

The queen's porter smiled triumphantly as he realized what he'd just overheard. He hurried back to the kingdom.

The next day, the little man arrived. Queen Sophia looked at the man and said, "Hello there, *Rumpelstiltskin*."

"That is impossible!" cried the man. "How did you know?"

Before hearing a reply, the man stomped with rage on the floor and fell right through, never to be heard from again.

In the end, Queen Sophia, the king, their little prince, and the miller all lived happily ever after.

Three Little Pigs

Illustrated by Susan Spellman
Adapted from James Orchard Halliwell-Phillipps' fairy tale

 hree little pigs set out to make their way in the world. They followed a path into the country until they came across a man who was selling straw. The first little pig bought all the straw the man had and built himself a little cottage on the edge of the meadow. No sooner had he settled in than a knock fell upon his door.

"Little pig! Little pig! Let me in!"
said a gruff voice. The pig peeked outside to
see a big, bad wolf standing there.

"Not by the hair on my chinny-chin-chin,"
squealed the pig.

"Then I'll huff, and I'll puff, and I'll blow
your house down!" said the big, bad wolf.

The wolf huffed, and he puffed, and
he blew the house down. The first
little pig scampered
quickly away.

Meanwhile, the
other two pigs were
still traveling along
the path.

The second little pig had met a man carrying a bundle of sticks, which the pig bought and used to build himself a lovely little cottage.

Just then, the big, bad wolf came along. He banged on the door, growling, "Little pig! Little pig! Let me in!"

"Not by the hair on my chinny-chin-chin!" said the second little pig.

"Then I'll huff, and I'll puff, and I'll blow your house down!" threatened the wolf.

And so he did. The second little pig ran away as his house tumbled to the ground.

The third little pig happened to meet a man carrying a load of bricks. This pig bought the man's bricks and built himself a very snug and sturdy little cottage that he was quite proud of.

It did not take long for the wolf to find the third pig. "Little pig! Little pig! Let me in!" growled the wolf.

"Not by the hair on my chinny-chin-chin!" squealed the third little pig.

"Then I'll huff, and I'll puff, and I'll blow your house down!" roared the wolf.

The wolf huffed, and he puffed, but he could not blow down the sturdy brick house.

The wolf quickly realized he would have to try to outsmart the pig. He saw the pig holding a turnip and came up with a plan. "Little pig," he said, "I see you like turnips. I bet you like juicy, sweet apples, too. There is a tree full of them up the road. I will show you at five o'clock tomorrow morning."

The little pig woke up at four o'clock and hurried off to find the apples.

Expecting the little pig to try and outsmart him, the wolf also awoke at four o'clock. Sure enough, the pig was already up in the tree, picking apples.

"I couldn't wait!" said the little pig. "Why don't you stand back? I will throw a delicious apple down to you."

The pig threw an apple as far as he could. While the wolf ran to find it, the little pig was able to scoot down the tree, scoop up some apples and scurry back home to safety.

Back at his little brick house, the pig made apple juice, applesauce, and apple pie. And naturally, the wolf came calling again.

"Little pig," said the wolf, "there is a fair in town today. Let us go together! I will come by to pick you up at three this afternoon."

The pig agreed. But, of course, he went much earlier than three.

The little pig was on his way home with a barrel he had won at the fair, when he saw the wolf approaching.

The smart little pig crawled into the barrel. He rocked it back and forth until it tipped over and began to roll down the hill. The barrel headed straight for the wolf! This frightened the wolf so much that he turned around and ran right home.

The next day, the wolf knocked on the little pig's door.

"Little pig," he said, "At three o'clock yesterday I was on my way to meet you at the fair, when the most frightening thing happened to me. It was simply awful!"

The little pig
laughed as the wolf
told the story of the
runaway barrel.

"I am afraid I
frightened you," said
the little pig. "I was in
the barrel!"

The wolf was very
angry to hear this.

"Little pig," roared the wolf, "I am going
to eat you for dinner today! I could not blow
your house down, and I could not trick you.
But now I will certainly come down the
chimney to get you!"

The little pig had hung a pot filled with water over the fire. The wolf tumbled down the chimney, right into the boiling water! The pig quickly put a heavy lid on the pot. And that was the end of the big, bad wolf.

Later that evening, there was a knock on the little pig's door. He was relieved to find his two brothers standing there. The three little pigs enjoyed turnip salad, warm apple pie, and a barrelful of applesauce. And they all lived happily ever after.

Snow White and the Seven Dwarves

Illustrated by Barbara Lanza
Adapted from the Grimm Brothers' fairy tale

Once upon a time, a beautiful princess named Snow White was born. Her mother died when Snow White was still just a baby. But after several years, the king was married again.

However, the woman he chose as his bride was very different from Snow White's mother.

The new queen was wicked and vain. She cared for nothing but her own beauty.

Every morning, the queen would visit her magic mirror and ask the same question: "Mirror, mirror, on the wall, who is the fairest one of all?"

The mirror replied, "You, my queen, are the fairest of all."

For years, the mirror gave the same answer to the queen's question. But then one day the queen visited the mirror and asked the usual question. This time, however, she received a different answer. "You, my queen, may have a beauty quite rare, but Snow White is a thousand times more fair."

Mad with jealousy, the queen sent for the royal huntsman.

She ordered him to take Snow White into the forest and kill her at once. Fearing for his own life, the huntsman took Snow White into the woods. When she looked up at him with her gentle eyes, full of trust, the huntsman could not bring himself to carry out the queen's order. Instead, he left Snow White in the forest and warned her never to return to the castle. The sky grew dark as Snow White wandered deep into the forest. She was terribly frightened, but continued onward.

Finally, Snow White found herself in a clearing beside a tiny cottage. She knocked, but there was no answer so she peeked inside. The cottage was cozy but untidy.

"Perhaps if I tidy this little cottage," she thought, "no one would mind if I have a bit of dinner and warm myself by the fire."

Snow White cleaned the cottage until it shone. Only then did she take a bit of bread. She sat down on one of the beds to wait for someone to come home. Snow White was so tired, and the bed was so cozy, that she soon fell fast asleep.

Some time later, Snow White awoke to find herself surrounded by seven kind faces. These seven dwarves, as they happened to be, welcomed her to their cottage and asked how she had found their home. Snow White told the dwarves about the evil queen and her flight through the dark forest.

The dwarves took pity on Snow White and invited her to stay with them.

Back at the castle, the evil queen gazed into her mirror and asked, "Mirror, mirror, on the wall, who is the fairest one of all?"

The mirror replied, "You, my queen, have a beauty quite rare, but beyond the great hill where the seven dwarves dwell, Snow White is thriving, and this I must tell: Within this realm she's still a thousand times more fair."

The queen flew into a rage and immediately set out to find Snow White. Then she disguised herself as a poor seamstress, calling out, "Gowns for sale!"

Snow White invited the seamstress into the cottage, where she tried on one of the dresses. The queen pulled the laces so tight that Snow White could not breathe, and she fell to the floor.

The dwarves came home that evening to find Snow White lying motionless on the ground. They quickly cut the laces that stifled her and, to their great relief, she breathed deeply and opened her eyes.

That night the queen triumphantly asked her mirror, "Mirror, mirror, on the wall, who is the fairest one of all?" The mirror replied with the same answer: Snow White was fairer than the queen.

Again in a rage, the angry queen wasted no time. She filled the teeth of her prettiest comb with a deadly poison. Then the queen disguised herself as a peddler and set out through the woods to the little cottage.

Snow White welcomed the peddler into the cottage. The queen selected the most beautiful comb and gently brushed Snow White's long, black hair. The moment the comb touched her head, Snow White fell to the ground.

When the dwarves returned home, they found Snow White on the floor. As they carried her to bed, the poisoned comb fell from her hair. Snow White was revived.

The queen returned to her mirror and said, "Mirror, mirror, on the wall, who is the fairest one of all?"

This time, the mirror answered simply, "Snow White is the fairest."

Yet again shaking with fury, the queen had another plan. She plucked an apple from the orchard and poisoned it. Then, disguised as a poor farmer woman, she set off.

"Apples for sale!" the queen called out. "These are the reddest and ripest apples in the kingdom."

Hearing the calls of the poor farmer woman, Snow White couldn't resist. She tried one of the apples.

She took one bite and fell to the ground. The queen smiled and slipped off into the woods, filled with satisfaction.

This time when the dwarves returned home, they could do nothing to wake Snow White. The dwarves wept for a long time before placing Snow White on a soft bed of flowers. They all believed that they would discover a way to revive Snow White, so they made sure that she had a comfortable bed to lie on as she dreamed sweetly in her deep sleep.

One day, a handsome prince rode through the forest and saw Snow White sleeping.

The dwarves told the prince about all that had happened. As the prince sat and listened, he stared at the peaceful Snow White. She was so beautiful! He couldn't explain it, but he had to give her a kiss.

No sooner did his lips leave hers than Snow White's eyes fluttered open, and she smiled up at the dashing prince. The curse was broken! A heartfelt kiss was all that was needed to break the queen's evil spell!

Within minutes, the prince asked Snow White to be his bride. She agreed happily!

A ceremony took place at the edge of the forest. The evil queen was seen lurking, but she quickly ran off, disappearing into the forest, never to be heard from again. Snow White and her prince, however, lived happily ever after!

The Frog Prince

Illustrated by Kathy Mitchell
Adapted from the Grimm Brothers' fairy tale

here once lived a great king who had a large family. One day, the king gave his daughter, Princess Annabel, a bouncy golden ball.

Princess Annabel loved to play with her golden ball. She would toss the ball into the air, catching it as it fell back down. It was a game she was quite good at—until the day she threw the ball too high. It bounced off of a tree branch and fell into a well.

The well was deep; Annabel's ball was gone forever. She was devastated.

"Please, don't cry," said a little voice.

Annabel looked around, but the only other creature in the garden was a frog. "Did you speak just now?" she said to the frog.

"Of course I did," said the frog. "I can get your ball if you'll do something for me."

"Would you like a kiss?" she asked.

"A kiss?" said the frog with a grimace. "No, thank you! All I want is for you to invite me to dinner tonight with your family."

"Certainly," said Princess Annabel.

The frog retrieved Annabel's golden ball with ease, and she invited him to dinner.

"What is this frog doing here?" asked the king as he arrived at the dinner table.

Annabel quickly explained.

"Very well," said the king. "If you made a promise, then you must keep your word."

No sooner had the first serving platter been placed on the table than the frog began to eat with messy delight. The family watched in amazement as the frog slurped and drooled all over the royal tablecloth.

"I hope you have left some room for dessert," Annabel said. After the kindness the frog had shown her, she wanted to be sure he enjoyed his meal. "Here, little frog, you have the first piece of cake."

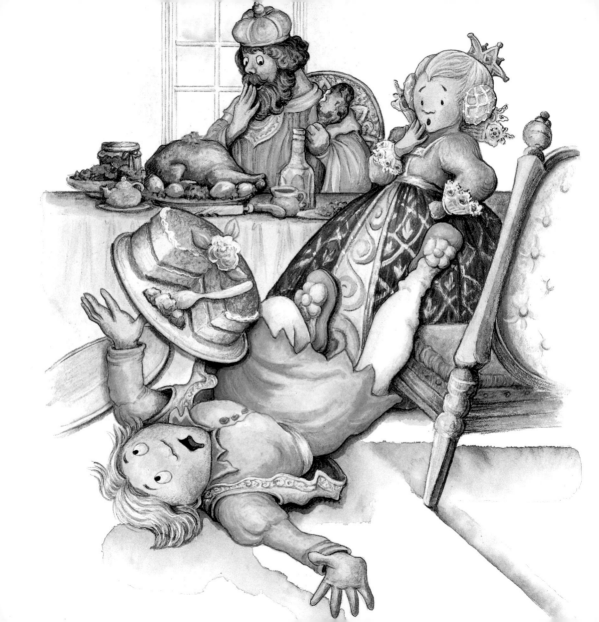

The frog looked up at her with wide eyes and a big smile. He ate his piece of cake in three bites.

Suddenly, a strange rumbling came from the frog's tummy. Princess Annabel and her father watched in disbelief as the little frog turned into a boy! A *prince!*

Annabel was in shock. She did not know what to think.

"I can explain," said the prince. "My name is Prince Harley. Many years ago, an evil witch cast a spell on me, making me a frog for all eternity. The only way the spell could be broken was for a princess to offer me a piece of cake from her dinner table."

Princess Annabel hardly knew what to say. She just stared at the young prince.

"I've been a frog for so many years," said Prince Harley. "I fully expected to be a frog forever. I am forever grateful for this meal."

"But you are so young," said Annabel.

"I was your age when the spell was cast," he said. "Once I became a frog, I never aged. I look the same today as when I was cursed. But I'm afraid that my family and friends are gone. Now I have nowhere to go."

The king decided to adopt Prince Harley.

"You shall live with us!" said the king. "We have more than enough room for you. And all the cake you can eat."

Prince Harley didn't know what to say. He was overjoyed. The prince absolutely loved his new family. He especially enjoyed playing catch with his new sister, Princess Annabel, and her golden ball. In the end, everyone lived happily ever after.

Thumbelina

Illustrated by Jane Maday
Adapted from the fairy tale by Hans Christian Andersen

nce there was a woman who lived alone in a tiny cottage. Though she had a happy life, she longed for a child.

One day as she worked in her yard, an old peddler woman came to her gate.

"I have something that can help you," the peddler told her kindly.

"Take these seeds and plant them in your garden," the woman continued. "In no time, you will find your heart's desire."

The woman thanked the peddler and planted the seeds. As soon as she watered them, a tulip sprouted up and instantly opened. Sitting in the flower was a beautiful little girl.

The woman decided to call the girl Thumbelina, and she loved and cared for her as her very own child.

One day while Thumbelina played in the garden, her sweet singing attracted an ugly toad who happened to be hopping by.

"I would like to make her my wife," he thought to himself. So he took Thumbelina and brought her to his lily pad.

Thumbelina was trapped, and she began sobbing. Her tears brought curious fish to the surface. They took pity on the poor girl, nibbled through the lily pad's stem, and helped her float safely to shore.

Thumbelina thanked the
fish for their help and set off
walking as far as her
legs could carry her,
but she did not know
where to find her
mother's garden. As
night fell, she wove
a tiny hammock
from blades of
grass, and slept.

The next
day, Thumbelina
resumed her search
for her mother.

Thumbelina's search went
on through the fall, and soon
winter brought a bitter cold chill
to the air. It was then that little
Thumbelina spotted a small
door in the trunk of a tree.
The door opened a
crack, and a little field
mouse peered out.
When the mouse
saw the lovely girl
on her doorstep,
she invited her in
to warm herself
by the fire.

The mouse and Thumbelina became fast friends, and Thumbelina, accepting the mouse's invitation to stay the winter, helped to gather food and supplies.

One day, a strange sound brought the field mouse and Thumbelina to the window. There they saw a sparrow with an injured wing. He had been traveling south for the winter, but now he could no longer fly. The sparrow knew he could not survive the cold winter outside.

The hospitable field mouse welcomed the sparrow into her home. Thumbelina helped him into the burrow and tried to make him as comfortable as possible.

The sparrow was surprised to see such a tiny person living with the field mouse.

"Are you a fairy princess?" he asked.

"What is a fairy?" she asked.

"Someday, when my wing is better, I will show you," answered the sparrow.

Thinking back to her mother's garden, Thumbelina asked if he was one of the birds that had taught her to sing.

"That was not me," said the sparrow. "But it could have been one of my brothers or sisters!"

Thumbelina and the sparrow would sing for their friend every day.

When spring finally arrived, the sparrow's wing had healed. He offered to carry Thumbelina to her mother's cottage. They both said their good-byes to the field mouse, and went on their way.

"I have a surprise for you, Thumbelina," said the sparrow as he landed on a flower. "I have brought you to the land where the fairies live."

Just then, a lovely white flower opened to reveal a perfect little boy the same size as Thumbelina! He had a pair of wings, and he wore a tiny crown. He was the prince of the fairies.

The prince asked Thumbelina to be his bride. He placed a golden crown on her head. Then two smaller fairies fastened a pair of delicate wings onto her back.

"I will marry you," she answered
happily. "But you and the fairies must come
live with me in my mother's garden. I will
never be happy anywhere else."

The prince agreed, and when they
arrived, the woman was overjoyed to see her
dear daughter again! She was
especially tickled to have
the fairies live with her.

Every summer the
sparrow would visit
Thumbelina's garden
where she and her
friends lived happily
ever after.

The Little Mermaid

Illustrated by John Martinez
Adapted from the fairy tale by Hans Christian Andersen

Deep in the ocean, a sea king lived in a castle made of coral. The sea king had six daughters. The youngest was the loveliest of all. She was quiet and thoughtful, and she had the most beautiful singing voice of all the mermaids.

On her twentieth birthday, each princess was allowed to visit the water's surface for the first time. Year after year, the little mermaid watched her older sisters take their turns. She couldn't wait for her birthday to come.

When the day finally arrived, she waved good-bye and rose swiftly to the surface. As her head rose above the top of the water, the little mermaid saw a large ship decorated with lights. A fancy celebration was underway.

The little mermaid swam closer
and saw a handsome young prince.
She watched him for a long time and
realized it was his birthday, too.

Just then, the wind began to blow
and the sky grew dark. Pounding
waves battered the prince's ship, and
she could hear it creak and groan.

Then, without warning, the prince
fell into the sea. The mermaid followed
him and used all of her
strength to pull the
prince safely
to shore.

Tenderly, the little mermaid brushed the hair from the prince's face and bent her head to kiss his forehead. When she heard excited shouts from the other end of the beach, she knew that she had to leave him.

For many days, the little mermaid could think of nothing but the prince.

"Perhaps the sea witch will agree to help you," suggested one of her older sisters.

The little mermaid went to visit the sea witch at once.

"Princess, I can give you human legs so you can walk and dance on land," she said. "But in return, you must give me your voice."

The little mermaid agreed to her terms.

The witch prepared the magic potion, then captured the little mermaid's voice, so the girl could neither speak nor sing.

The little mermaid swam to the surface and drank the potion without hesitation. She felt quite strange, and her tail began to ache. Then, before her eyes, her tail transformed into two human legs!

The prince was on his morning walk when he discovered the beautiful, silent girl on the beach. Not knowing how else to help her, he brought her with him to the palace.

The girl used her graceful movements and expressive eyes to speak to those around her. She danced and glided on her new legs.

153

Everyone in the palace was enchanted by the little mermaid, especially the prince. He felt as if he had met her before.

Everywhere the prince went, the little mermaid was by his side. They rode together on horseback through the sweet-scented woods. As the days passed, the little mermaid fell deeper and deeper in love with the prince. As it happened, he also grew very fond of her.

The little mermaid loved to stroll through the gardens of the palace, hand in hand with the prince.

But at night, when the royal household was asleep, the little mermaid would follow the broad marble steps from the palace down to the water's edge. There she would sit in the moonlight and bathe her weary feet in the cool sea water. Her thoughts would turn to her beloved family.

One night, her sisters rose to the surface, singing as they floated on the water. They saw the little mermaid and swam closer. They told her how much they missed her. They pleaded with her to return with them to their home beneath the sea.

The little mermaid smiled at them. She used gestures to explain how wonderful it was to be with the prince.

After that, her sisters came to the palace every night to visit.

She even saw her father once, in the distance. He had not been to the surface in many years and did not venture so near the land as her sisters.

Then one afternoon the little mermaid learned that the king and queen wanted the prince to marry a princess of a nearby kingdom. The little mermaid felt a sudden chill. Would the prince really choose to marry another?

At the thought, her expressive eyes became brilliant with tears. Yet she still smiled at the prince.

The prince reached for the little mermaid's hand. When she turned to him, she saw a look of love.

Could her dream be coming true?

"Mother and Father," said the prince, "my true love is here. I desire no other."

The prince sank to one knee and looked into the little mermaid's eyes. "Will you marry me?" he asked her.

Unexpectedly, the little mermaid's voice returned to her. Their love had broken the sea witch's spell!

"Yes!" she exclaimed.

Soon after, the prince and the little mermaid were wed in a magnificent ceremony. As they sailed away, the newlyweds waved farewell.

The new couple sailed around the world. And naturally, everyone lived happily ever after.

The End